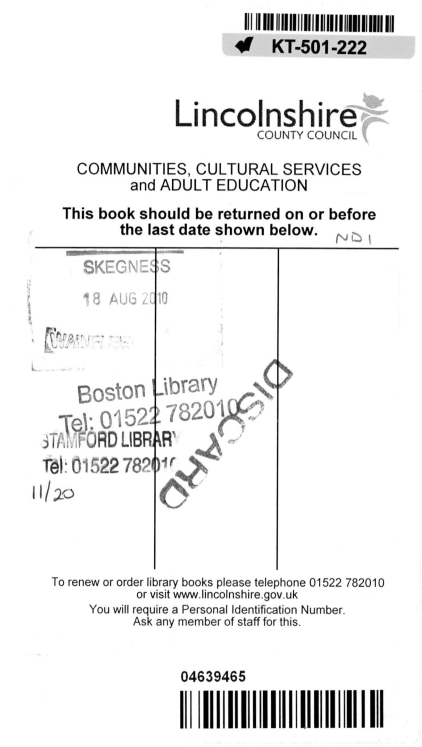

You can read the stories in the
Greek Beasts and Heroes series in any order.

If you'd like to read more about some of
the characters in this book, turn to pages
78 and 79 to find out which other books to try.

Atticus's journey continues on
from *The Dragon's Teeth*.

To find out where he goes next,
read *The One-Eyed Giant*.

GREEK BEASTS AND HEROES

The Hero's Spear

LUCY COATS
Illustrated by Anthony Lewis

Orion
Children's Books

Text and illustrations first appeared in
Atticus the Storyteller's 100 Greek Myths
First published in Great Britain in 2002
by Orion Children's Books
This edition published in Great Britain in 2010
by Orion Children's Books
a division of the Orion Publishing Group Ltd
Orion House
5 Upper St Martin's Lane
London WC2H 9EA
An Hachette UK company

1 3 5 7 9 8 6 4 2

The Orion Publishing Group's policy is to use papers that are natural,
renewable and recyclable products and made from wood grown in sustainable
forests. The logging and manufacturing processes are expected to conform
to the environmental regulations of the country of origin.

A catalogue record for this book is available from the British Library

ISBN 978 1 4440 0074 0

Printed in China

www.orionbooks.co.uk
www.lucycoats.com

For Hero (of course), Sika, Teasel and Willow,
and in memory of Otter, Pipkin and little Sophy,
faithful dogs every one.
L. C.

For Bertha
A. L.

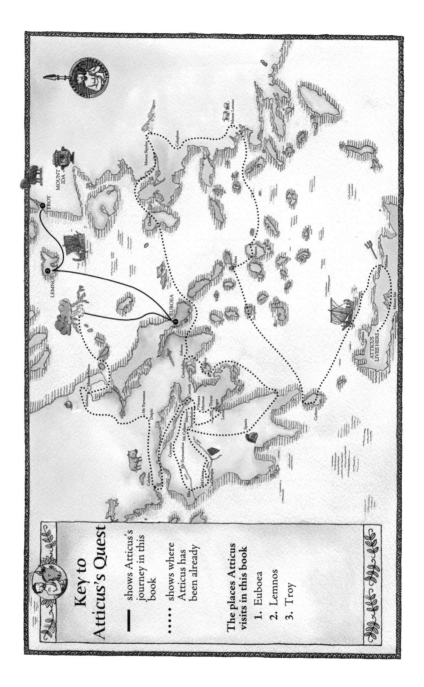

Key to
Atticus's Quest

— shows Atticus's
    journey in this
    book

⋯⋯⋯ shows where
    Atticus has
    been already

**The places Atticus
visits in this book**

1. Euboea
2. Lemnos
3. Troy

Contents

Stories from the Heavens

Long ago, in ancient
Greece, gods and
goddesses, heroes and
heroines lived together with
fearful monsters and every kind of
fabulous beast that ever
flew, or walked or swam.
But little by little, as people
began to build more villages
and towns and cities, the gods and
monsters disappeared into
the secret places of the world
and the heavens, so that they
could have some peace.

9

Before they
disappeared, the gods
and goddesses gave
the gift of storytelling
to men and women, so that nobody
would ever forget them. They ordered
that there should be a great storytelling
festival once every seven years on the
slopes of Mount Ida, near Troy, and that
tellers of tales should come from all over
Greece and from lands near and far to

 take part. Every seven
years a beautiful painted
vase, filled to the brim
with gold, magically
appeared as a first prize, and the winner
was honoured for the rest of his life by
all the people of Greece.

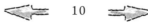

The wind had got up, and the sails were flapping in a worrying way. Atticus huddled beside Melissa as sailors scurried about the ship.

"Looks like we're in for a summer storm," shouted Captain Nikos as he wrestled with the rudder. "Best stay down where you are."

Melissa's ears drooped miserably as the boat tossed. Atticus patted her.

"Don't worry, old girl, Nikos is a good sailor. He'll get us through this. I'll tell you a story to take your mind off the weather."

The Greeks' Bargain

Helen of Sparta had skin like a perfect peach and long dark hair that shone like a raven's wing. Her lips were the deep red of rose petals and when she smiled the people around her would shade their eyes and look to see if the sun had come out.

Every prince in Greece was madly in love with her, and when she was old enough to be married, they all brought rich gifts to tempt her into choosing one of them as her husband.

Tyndareus, her stepfather, would not let her accept any of the presents.

"We don't want them to think you have any favourites, my dear," he said wisely.

In private, though, Tyndareus was worried. Every night he tossed and turned beside his wife, Leda, as he tried to think of a way to choose a husband for Helen without offending any of the other princes.

"It can't be done," he said despairingly.

But the next morning Odysseus came to see him. Odysseus was the king of Ithaca, the son of Sisyphus Sharp-Eyes,

and the grandson of Autolyus the cattle thief, and he was very cunning. He knew he wasn't rich or powerful enough to marry Helen himself, and anyway, he was in love with a girl called Penelope. But Penelope's father didn't like him one bit.

"If I help you to find a way of finding a husband for Helen without offending anyone," he said, "will you help me to marry Penelope?"

Tyndareus said yes at once. He knew how clever Odysseus was.

"This is what you have to do," said Odysseus. "Give Helen a golden wreath, and blindfold her. Then make the suitors all stand in a circle around her. Turn her around three times, and then make her walk towards them. Whoever she crowns first will be her husband."

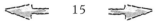

"But the ones who have to go away will still be offended," said Tyndareus nervously.

"Ah!" laughed Odysseus. "But this is the clever part. Before Helen chooses you must make the suitors swear an unbreakable oath to support her choice and to defend her husband against anyone who takes her away from him. That way, no one can be upset or all the others will be against him."

Tyndareus agreed that this was a brilliant idea, and the very next day he carried out the plan.

When the kings and princes had promised in front of the gods themselves to support Helen's future husband, Helen was blindfolded and given a golden wreath.

"Oh goddess of love, please let me crown Menelaus," she whispered under her breath, and Aphrodite heard her.

Suddenly, a tiny pinprick of light appeared before Helen's eyes. Aphrodite had made a secret hole in the blindfold.

"One!" shouted the men in the circle.

"Two!" as Helen was twirled and whirled around.

"Three!" as she staggered and nearly fell with dizziness.

As she regained her balance, she walked straight towards the handsome prince of her dreams and put the wreath onto his head.

Menelaus and Helen were married at once, and after Tyndareus died, Menelaus became king of Sparta. After the wedding the kings and princes went back to their homes, but in their hearts each secretly hoped never to be called on to fulfil their great oath.

Little did they know that the gods themselves had planned for them to have to.

Lightning flashed, and thunder crashed overhead. The sails were now lashed tight to the mast, and Captain Nikos and his crew were struggling to steer the ship away from the shore.

Atticus spat out a mouthful of seawater as the wind roared and howled around the ship. He was kneeling with his arm around Melissa, who was lying on the deck, her eyes wide with fear. Atticus felt a tap on his back. It was the ship's boy.

"I'm so frightened, Atticus," he whimpered.

"Me too," said Atticus. "But these summer storms soon blow over. I'll tell you a story to pass the time."

The Face That Launched a Thousand Ships

Priam, king of Troy, opened his arms wide. "My dear son," he said, tears trickling down his cheeks. "Can you ever forgive me? Welcome home." And he gave Paris a big hug.

Just then there was a commotion at a nearby window.

"Woe!" shrieked a girl's voice. "Woe to Troy! I see death and war and disaster!"

"Who on earth is that?" asked Paris nervously.

"Oh, that's just our sister Cassandra," said his brother Hector. "We never take any notice of her, she's always moaning on.

Thinks she can see into the future or something."

Paris had arrived in Troy the day before. He had been determined to attend the great games held every year in honour of the son King Priam had sent off to be murdered by his chief herdsman. Priam had felt guilty about his dreadful deed ever since.

"I think it's time that murdered son came back to life," Paris said to his foster father Agelaus.

But Agelaus had shaken his head.
"You have your wonderful bulls, what
more do you want?" he asked.

And when he had gone to Oenone's
fountain to say goodbye, she had clung to
him, crying. "If you are ever wounded,

come back to me. I am the only one who can heal you," she sobbed as he strode off.

Paris had entered every event in the games, and won them all.

"Who is this magnificent young man?" whispered the crowd. "Surely he must be a prince."

As Paris came forward to collect his winner's crown from King Priam, Agelaus had stepped out of the crowd. "Your Majesty," he cried. "Forgive me! This is your long-lost son, returned from the dead. I didn't kill him after all."

And Priam had wept with joy at the news.

"Better that Troy is destroyed than that I should lose my beloved son again," he said to the priests who reminded him of the old prophecy that Paris would one day bring disaster to the city.

Paris was popular with everyone, and soon his father was talking about finding him a wife.

Paris just laughed. "Only the best in Greece will do for me," he said, remembering Aphrodite's promise to him.

A few nights later Aphrodite came to him in secret. "King Menelaus is arriving in Troy tomorrow," she said. "Ask to go with him to Sparta, and then I will arrange for his wife Helen to fall in love with you. You can escape back to Troy with her, and then you will be married."

Paris was very excited. He couldn't wait to see the famous Helen.

He pretended to make friends with Menelaus at once, and begged him to let him visit Sparta.

"I have heard so much about your famous city, and I would love to come and see it," he lied.

Menelaus agreed, and soon they had set sail. Priam had given Paris a beautiful ship with a figurehead of Aphrodite on the prow, and the goddess sent gentle breezes to help them on their way.

The palace at Sparta was huge and impressive with blood-red walls and heavy golden gates which opened with a blast of trumpets as Menelaus and Paris approached.

"Behold the king!" cried a herald as a tall woman came running out. She ran to Menelaus and flung her arms around him. "I am so glad you're back, dear husband," she said. "I have missed you so much."

Paris's mouth fell open at his first sight of Helen. She was definitely the most beautiful woman he had ever seen, although he didn't think he would tell Aphrodite that.

That night, after a wonderful welcome feast, Aphrodite made her son Eros invisible and sent him to shoot one of his love darts into Helen's heart.

Although she had loved Menelaus ever since she could remember, the minute the dart touched Helen's skin she could think of nothing and nobody but Paris.

"Dear prince," she whispered, as she passed him in the corridor. "Take me away from this horrible place. I can't think why I ever married that stupid Menelaus!"

So later that night Paris knocked at Helen's door, and disguised in thick black cloaks, they galloped through the night, sneaked aboard his ship and set sail.

"I will never let you go," he vowed as he kissed her. "Not if all the kings of Greece come knocking at the gates of Troy."

When Menelaus discovered where Helen had gone, he was furious.

"I'll teach that Trojan rogue to steal my wife!" he roared, stomping round the throne room in a rage. "Send messengers to all the kings and princes. It is time for them to keep the promises they made when I married her. I shall launch a thousand ships to get her back! We will go to war!"

And he went off to order his army and his fleet to make ready.

The sky was washed clean of clouds and the sun shone brightly over the ship as its sails filled with the brisk south-westerly wind.

"Perfect!" shouted Captain Nikos. "We shall be at Troy in no time with this breeze!"

Atticus leant over the side, watching the clear blue water slip by

"Did I ever tell you how Odysseus nearly didn't go to Troy?" he asked Melissa.

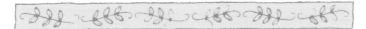

The King Who Ploughed Sand

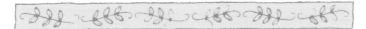

King Menelaus and his herald, the hero Palamedes, rode the length and breadth of Greece calling up the kings and princes to war.

Tantara, tantara, tantara, called the great brass trumpet, as Menelaus landed on the island of Ithaca, and set off towards Odysseus's palace.

Now Odysseus was as cunning as a thousand weasels and as slippery as a bucketful of eels. He didn't want to keep his promise to Menelaus and go to war at all, because Zeus's oracle had once told him that if he did, the gods wouldn't let him return for twenty years, and that when he did come back he would be a beggar.

Odysseus didn't want to leave his comfortable palace and full wine cellar, and he certainly didn't want to spend twenty years away from his beautiful wife, Penelope, and his little son Telemachus.

"You must lie for me," he hissed at Penelope as he ran out of the back door. "Tell them I've gone mad and am doing something strange on the beach and can't come."

He went quickly to a shepherd's hut and changed into some dirty, ragged old clothes and a stupid-looking pink felt hat shaped like half an egg. Then he led a great big ox and a tiny little donkey down to the field at the edge of the beach and harnessed them to an old plough.

Menelaus and Palamedes were very angry when they heard why Odysseus was not at home.

"Mad?" roared Menelaus. "He's no more mad than I am! Take us to him at once."

So Penelope bundled Telemachus into a sling and led them down to the beach.

As they got nearer they heard a strange song being sung in a high, cracked voice.

"Plant the seaweed,
Make it grow,
Plough the sand
When tides are low ..."

And there was Odysseus skipping and singing up and down the beach, throwing handfuls of salt over his shoulder as he tried to plough a straight furrow with the ox and the donkey. He wasn't doing a very good job of it. When Odysseus saw Penelope, Menelaus and Palamedes approaching, he stopped and leaned on the plough handle.

"Ooh! Fine strangers to see poor little Odysseus plan his seaweed!" he giggled, rolling his eyes madly. "And who might you be, lovely lady?"

Menelaus stamped his foot.

"Stop this silliness at once and come and keep your promise to me!" he growled.

But Odyssues just danced a little jig and carried on ploughing.

"Right! said Palamedes. "I've had enough of this. Let's see if he really is mad and doesn't recognise us."

He snatched Telemachus out of Penelope's arms and laid him down in the path of the plough. On and on came the stamping hooves, but just at the last minute Odysseus pulled on the reins and stopped them. He ran to pick up his son.

"All right, Palamedes," he said. "I accept my fate. You win."

And he went to order his soldiers and his warships to make ready.

So Odysseus and his fleet went to join

the other Greek kings at Aulis. He kissed Penelope and Telemachus with tears running down his cheeks.

"Never forget me," he begged. "And however long it takes for me to return, you will wait for me, won't you?"

Penelope promised that she would – but she never guessed how hard it would be for her to keep that promise in the long, empty years to come.

After they had made their sacrifice of wine and salt, the sailors sat down to eat their soggy bread and olives.

"How about a story, Atticus?" said Nikos.

"I'll tell you how the Greek fleet got stuck in Aulis, just over there," said Atticus, pointing west over the hills.

The Sacrifice of a Princess

Menelaus's Greek fleet of a thousand ships had just gathered near Aulis for the second time.

Many delays and false starts had prevented them from setting off before. Odysseus was there, with his men of Ithaca, so was Achilles with his best friend Patroclus and their soldiers, together with many other kings, princes and heroes.

The captains of the fleet were King Agamemnon, Menelaus's brother, and King Idomeneus of Crete.

"Let us start at once, my brothers!"

cried Agamemnon from the deck of his great fighting galley. "Forward to Troy!"

There was a huge cheer as the sails were raised, and the mass of ships moved forward. But as they reached the mouth of the harbour a strong wind rose up from the north-east and drove them back.

It blew and blew and blew for days and days, until Agamemnon thought they would never be able to leave.

He called for his soothsayer, Calchas. "Tell us what to do, old man," he commanded.

So Calchas cast his magic stones and muttered and mumbled as he looked for an answer from the gods.

Finally he looked up. "You have offended the goddess Artemis," he said in his wheezy voice. "You must sacrifice

the prettiest of your daughters to her,
or you will never get away."

Agamemnon was horrified. "Sacrifice
my daughter, Iphigenia?" he cried.
"What will my wife Clytemnestra say?"

But when the Greek kings heard
the news, they insisted that Iphigenia
be sent for.

"We won't go to war with you if you don't," they said.

So poor Iphigenia was brought to Aulis to be sacrificed. She was very frightened, but very brave, and as she stood on the altar in her simple white dress, Agamemnon wept as he watched and had to be dragged away.

"I am doing this freely, for my father, for the goddess and for Greece," Iphigenia said as she bared her graceful neck for the axe.

Now Artemis loved brave people, and so she flew down at once in a cloud of silver raindrops and seized Iphigenia away to safety just as the axe fell.

At that minute, the wind dropped and began to blow in the right direction.

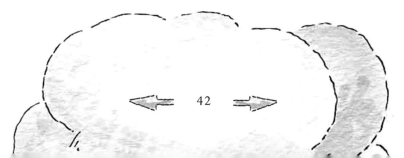

The kings and their men whooped
as they ran back to the ships and set sail
immediately.

"Trojans beware!" bellowed King
Agamemnon joyfully as he jumped aboard.
"The Greeks are coming to get you!"

They landed on Lemnos two days later.
Captain Nikos decided to spend a few
days on the island repairing the rudder,
which had been damaged in the storm.

"Can't sail up the Hellespont with no
rudder," he said grimly. "Too dangerous."

Melissa wobbled off the boat thankfully
- a donkey's legs are not meant for sea
journeys, and she wanted grass. She and
Atticus wandered off to explore.

The Smelly Wound

When Heracles had died and gone up to Olypmus to live with the gods, he had given his great bow and arrows to the man who had lit his funeral pyre, a young man called Philoctetes. Philoctetes was almost as strong as Heracles himself, so although no other man on earth could use the bow, Philoctetes had no trouble in drawing the string back to his shoulder.

"It's as easy as eating cherries," he boasted, and when Menelaus's call to war went out, Philoctetes was one of the first to join up.

"You'll need me before this is all over, I expect," he said. "After all, I am the greatest archer in all Greece."

So as the Greek fleet set sail at last, Philoctetes and his bow went with them. Soon they came to a little island, where they stopped to take on water.

"Just going to stretch my legs," said Philoctetes, leaping out onto the shore.

But he didn't look before he jumped down, and he landed on a horrible poisonous snake, which bit him on the foot.

"Aaargh!" he screamed, thrashing and crashing around with the pain.

His friends soon came running, and they cut a cross between the fang marks and sucked out the poison. But they didn't suck out all of it, and soon Philoctetes' foot was swollen to the size of a football.

The ships sailed on towards Troy, but as they got nearer and nearer, Philoctetes' wound began to get smellier and smellier. Soon everyone in the fleet was holding their noses against the terrible stench.

Just outside the entrance to the Hellespont lies the island of Lemnos, and it was there that the kings and captains decided to leave poor Philoctetes all by himself to get better.

"We really can't have him with us," they whispered. "He just smells too disgusting."

So at the dead of night they lifted Philoctetes into a little boat, together with some food and water and his precious bow and arrows and rowed him out to the island, where they dumped him on the beach.

By this time he was feeling too ill to care about anything, but in a week the wound began to crust over, and although it still smelled disgusting, Philoctetes could hobble about enough to catch food and find water. He was very cross at being left behind, but there was nothing he could do.

He never guessed that it would be nearly ten years before he saw his friends again, and that his wound would still be as smelly as ever when he did.

But that is quite another story.

They had just landed at the harbour near Troy and Atticus had butterflies in his stomach. He and Melissa got off the ship and walked into a jostling mass of people.

"This way for the storytelling festival!" a man was shouting.

Captain Nikos was busy supervising the unloading of his cargo, but he had promised Atticus that he and the crew would come and see him perform.

Now Atticus had to register for the competition. There was a long queue.

"We'll just have to wait," he muttered to Melissa. "I'll tell you a story very quietly, to keep me calm."

The Cunning Plan

Although the Greek kings had many men, horses and weapons, they hadn't been able to bring enough provisions for a whole army.

So before they attacked the city of Troy itself, they first had to conquer all the cities and towns and farmland around it so that they could feed themselves.

It took them nine long years of fighting and effort, and at the end of it even the heroes among them were weary and longing for home.

But at last they reached the Great Plain of Troy and set up camp. Then from the tops of their crowded ramparts

the people of Troy could see huge amounts of stores and horses and armour hidden behind the high wall that the Greeks had built to protect their ships from the Trojan army.

A thousand tents and a thousand banners flapped in the breeze, and the smoke of a thousand campfires swirled and whirled in the air, bringing wafts of cooking meat and simmering beans to the worried citizens.

"We are doomed,"wailed Cassandra, King Priam's daughter. "Doomed!"

But as usual no one took any notice of her.

King Priam and his counsellors were in the throne room, having a meeting.

"We must send for our ally King Rhesus at once," said King Priam.

"The priests have just reminded me of a prophecy. It says that once his white horses have drunk from the River Scamander, Troy will stand for ever and ever. No one will be able to beat us." So a messenger was sent, and soon the news came that King Rhesus, his horses and his army were on their way.

Now King Menelaus had just captured a Trojan spy called Dolon.

Dolon was a terrible coward, so he had told Menelaus all about the prophecy.

"We must stop these horses drinking from the river," said Menelaus, and he sent for Odysseus and his friend Diomedes at once. "Think of a cunning plan," he begged them.

Cunning plans were what Odysseus was best at, and soon he had come up with a brilliant one.

He and Diomedes sneaked past the enemy sentries at dead of night and killed King Rhesus as he slept in his tent. Then they stole his beautiful white horses.

Tiptoeing out of the enemy camp, they put them onto a ship and sent it far, far away.

The horses never drank a drop from the River Scamander, and as their master was dead, the prophecy never came true.

"I really am the most cunning man in the world," said Odysseus gleefully as he and Diomedes celebrated their success. However, the Greeks would need a lot more than cunning to win the war and return Helen to her husband.

By the time Atticus had settled Melissa and found a corner to sleep in he was tired.

"Two hundred competitors so far, and more coming in all the time," he yawned. "How will they manage to hear all of us?"

The next morning he and Melissa walked towards the walls of Troy with Callimachus, a boy who had slept beside them the night before. Callimachus had travelled all the way from Cyrene in Libya to come to the Festival, and he had been begging Atticus to tell him a story ever since they woke up.

"'Good fortune will come from Cyrene's son,'" Atticus remembered.

"I wonder if the oracle at Delphi meant that this boy is going to bring me luck?"

The Hero's Spear

The Greeks shivered and shook and groaned behind their high wall.

The war had not been going at all well, and now they had all been struck down by a terrible plague, which gave them boils in nasty places and hot horrible headaches which felt as if monsters were trampling their skulls.

It was all King Agamemnon's fault. He had stolen a beautiful girl named Chryseis from her father, a priest of Apollo, and made her into his slave. This had annoyed the god, and so he had begun to shoot his dreadful Plague Arrows into the Greek camp.

"That will soon make Agamemnon give her back," Apollo said to Chryseis's father, who had come to him for help.

Now Chryseis had a friend called Briseis who had been captured at the same time. Agamemnon had given Briseis to Achilles as a present, but when he found that the only way to stop the plague was to give Chryseis back to her father, he went to Achilles' tent and took his gift back.

"Sorry, old chap," he said. "But you don't really need her, do you?" This made Achilles so angry that he stomped into his tent and refused to come out, even when the fighting got really fierce and the Trojans started winning.

"I shan't put on even one piece of armour till Agamemnon apologises," he muttered to his best friend Patroclus.

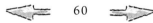

Patroclus loyally stayed with Achilles in the hot stuffy tent all that day and night, but finally, as dawn broke, and he heard the clash of swords and spears begin the battle again, he couldn't bear it any longer.

"Look, Achilles," he said, "the Trojans are trying to burn Ajax's ships, and – oh no! Diomedes and Odysseus are both wounded. We must go and help them!"

Achilles just turned his back. "Serves them right!" he mumbled. But as the day went on, he began to feel guilty, as more and more of his friends were wounded or killed. Patroclus finally persuaded Achilles to lend him his golden armour and helmet, and to let him lead Achilles' troops out to help the Greeks.

"The Trojans will think it's you," he said. "It'll be funny to see how fast they run away!"

As Patroclus and his men charged towards them, the Trojans began to panic.

"Oh no! It's Achilles the Awful!" they cried, as they flung down their weapons.

Only their leader, Prince Hector, stood firm.

When Patroclus came near him, followed by the whole Greek army, he raised his spear and flung it at Hector. But the spear clanged on Hector's shield and fell uselessly to the ground.

As Achilles stood outside his tent and watched, Hector's own great spear sailed through the air and hit Patroclus with a deadly blow.

Patroclus fell to the ground, and Achilles knew that his best friend in the whole world was dead. He began to tear his hair and wail.

"Oh why, why, why did I let him go?"
he screamed, and then he shook his fist
at the Trojans, who were retreating,
carrying the golden armour that
Patroclus had borrowed.

That night, Achilles asked his mother
Thetis to get him some new armour, and
by morning the god Hephaestus had
forged him a suit like nothing that has
ever been made before or since.

It was all of gold and silver, with pictures of gods and battles so cunningly hammered into the metal that the figures looked quite alive.

"I hope you're ready for me, Hector," said Achilles grimly, as he went to sharpen his sword and spear for the battle ahead. "Because I'm coming to kill you."

Atticus was surprised at how small old Troy actually was. Although there were now new houses and hovels scattered higgledy-piggledy around it, the citadel itself was tiny.

Atticus stood under the Great Gate, holding Melissa's rope, and looked admiringly at the thick walls.

"I understand now how Achilles was able to chase Hector three times round the city boundary," he said to Callimachus. "I always wondered about that."

"Tell me the story," said Callimachus eagerly.

Revenge!

Before he went out to fight against Hector, Achilles made peace with Agamemnon. The great king came out of his tent, wild-haired and red-eyed from weeping all night for the many heroes who had died or been wounded in battle the day before.

He held out his arms and Achilles embraced him silently. Then Agamemnon gave the slave-girl Briseis back to Achilles, together with gifts of gold and jewels.

"Friends should not fight," he said hoarsely. "Will you forgive me?"

And then Achilles wept too, great silver tears that ran down his armour like a bright river.

Just then the sun rose from behind the dark hills, and the battle trumpets began to sound.

"To war!" cried Achilles, leaping into his chariot and thundering off across the plain with all that was left of the Greek army running and yelling behind.

It was a terrifying sight, but Hector of Troy was a brave man. All his troops had fled once more at the sight of Achilles, so he stood alone in front of the Great Gate of Troy.

As Achilles came nearer and nearer
he raised the golden spear that had killed
Patroclus, and began to charge.

As he ran, he flung the spear as hard
as he could, but Achilles' new shield had
so much magic in it that the spear
bounced off harmlessly.

Then Hector drew his sword and
tried to leap into the chariot beside
Achilles. But Achilles leaped out of the
chariot, and started to chase him round
the city walls.

Three times round they went, slashing and stabbing at each other, until at last the two heroes were so out of breath that they stopped once more before the Great Gate of Troy.

Then Achilles raised his spear high above his head, and as he lunged forward and stabbed Hector in the chest he cried out.

"Hear me, my Patroclus! Your death is avenged!"

Hector sank down dying to the bare brown earth, and Achilles bent over him in triumph.

"I shall leave your wretched body here for the wolves and eagles to tear!" he hissed.

But Hector opened both his eyes very wide and looked Achilles in the face.

"Let my father pay gold to get my body back, so that I can be buried in my beloved Troy," he gasped. "If you do not, then you will die here, before this very gate. Remember me when the arrow flies . . ."

Then he fell back dead.

Not a bird sang, not a sword rattled, not a speck of dust moved – all was as still and silent as if the gods themselves were listening.

A great scream of anger and grief went up from the high walls of Troy as Achilles tied the dead Hector's heels to his chariot, and dragged his body all round the battlefield, round and round and round and round.

At last, as night fell, the Great Gate opened and an old man stepped out, dressed all in rags, with dust all over his grey head and beard. As he walked

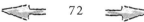

through the dusk towards the Greek
camp, they saw that he was carrying a
sign of peace.

"What do you want, old man," said
Achilles roughly, as he approached the
chariot, where Hector's body lay
sprawled in the dirt.

"I am Priam, king of Troy," the old man whispered sadly. "I have come for my son's body, so that I can bury him as a prince deserves. Let me take him home."

But Achilles was still so angry with Hector for killing Patroclus, that he refused.

"The only way you will get him, your Majesty, is to bring me his bodyweight in gold. Until then he shall lie here in the dust where he belongs."

Priam trudged wearily back to Troy and opened up his treasury.

There was not much left in it. So he asked his people to help. Soon a heavy blanketful of gold was heaped on the ground beside Hector's body, which was now lying in a huge sling, on one side of an enormous pair of scales.

"Let's see if it's enough!" said Achilles.
"Throw the gold onto the other side."

Slowly, slowly, Hector's body rose up,
but as the last piece of gold was tipped in,
the scales were not quite even.

A groan went up from the Trojans,
but just then a girl stepped forward.
It was Polyxena, Hector's sister.

"Here, dearest brother," she said softly. "Take my rings and bracelets. I don't need them now."

As Polyxena's jewellery fell with a clink onto the heap, the scales levelled.

"Enough!" roared Achilles. "Take the body!"

But as the silent, solemn procession marched slowly back to Troy, his eyes could only see one thing – Polyxena's beautiful sad face.

Achilles buried his face in his hands and wept as he realised that he had fallen in love with the sister of the man he had just killed.

Greek Beasts and Heroes and where to find them ...

Odysseus's father was Sisyphus – who was almost as clever as his legendary son. Would you like to meet "The Sharp-Eyed King"? You can find his story in *The Dolphin's Message*.

Poor Helen didn't have a chance of living happily ever after once Aphrodite had decided to break up her marriage to

Menelaus. You can find out what the naughty goddess of love planned in a story called "The Fairest Goddess" in *The Dragon's Teeth*.

Priam wept for joy when his long-lost son was returned to him, but Daedelus was not nearly so lucky. The story of his son – "The Boy Who Fell Out of the Sky" – is one of the most famous ever told, and you can read it in *The Beasts in the Jar.*

Poor Iphigenia was sacrificed in this book. Which princess was about to be sacrificed to the god Poseidon? And which hero saved her? Read "The Magic Head", in the book of that title, to find out!

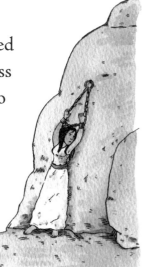